Franklin's Picnic

From an episode of the animated TV series *Franklin*,
produced by Nelvana Limited, Neurones France s.a.r.l. and
Neurones Luxembourg S.A, based on the Franklin books
by Paulette Bourgeois and Brenda Clark.

Story written by Sharon Jennings.

Illustrated by Sean Jeffrey, Sasha McIntyre and Shelley Southern.

Based on the TV episode *Franklin's Picnic*, written by Brian Lasenby.

 Kids Can Read is a registered trademark of Kids Can Press Ltd.

Franklin

Franklin is a trademark of Kids Can Press Ltd.
The character of Franklin was created by Paulette Bourgeois and Brenda Clark.
Text © 2006 Contextx Inc.
Illustrations © 2006 Brenda Clark Illustrator Inc.

Kids Can Press acknowledges the financial support of the Government of Ontario,
through the Ontario Media Development Corporation's Ontario Book Initiative; the
Ontario Arts Council; the Canada Council for the Arts; and the Government of
Canada, through the BPIDP, for our publishing activity.

Published in Canada by
Kids Can Press Ltd.
29 Birch Avenue
Toronto, ON M4V 1E2

Published in the U.S. by
Kids Can Press Ltd.
2250 Military Road
Tonawanda, NY 14150

www.kidscanpress.com

Series editor: Tara Walker
Edited by Jennifer Stokes
Designed by Céleste Gagnon

Printed and bound in China

The hardcover edition of this book is smyth sewn casebound.
The paperback edition of this book is limp sewn with a drawn-on cover.

CM 06 0 9 8 7 6 5 4 3 2 1
CM PA 06 0 9 8 7 6 5 4 3 2 1

Library and Archives Canada Cataloguing in Publication Data

Jennings, Sharon
   Franklin's picnic / Sharon Jennings ; illustrated by Sean Jeffrey, Sasha McIntyre, Shelley Southern.

(Kids Can read)
The character Franklin was created by Paulette Bourgeois and Brenda Clark.

ISBN-13: 978-1-55337-714-6 (bound).   ISBN-13: 978-1-55337-715-3 (pbk.)
ISBN-10: 1-55337-714-1 (bound).   ISBN-10: 1-55337-715-X (pbk.)

I. Jeffrey, Sean   II. McIntyre, Sasha III. Southern, Shelley
IV. Bourgeois, Paulette V. Clark, Brenda VI. Title. VII. Series: Kids Can read (Toronto, Ont.)

PS8569.E563F765 2006   jC813'.54   C2004-906886-5

Kids Can Press is a  Entertainment company

Franklin's Picnic

Kids Can Press

Franklin can tie his shoes.

Franklin can count by twos.

And Franklin can eat

lots of flies.

Franklin loves flies.

Franklin's friends do not love flies.

Sometimes, this is a problem.

One day, Franklin was playing baseball.

It was his turn at bat.

"Uh-oh," said Bear. "It's twelve o'clock.

I have to go home for lunch."

"Me too," said Skunk.

"Me too," said everyone else.

"Wait till I have my turn!" cried Franklin.

But his friends all ran off.

"Phooey," said Franklin.

7

Franklin went home

and ate lunch by himself.

Then he ran back to the park

and waited for his friends.

He waited ...

... and waited.

By the time everyone showed up,

Franklin had a good idea.

"Let's eat lunch together tomorrow," he said.

"You mean a picnic?" asked Beaver.

"Yes," said Franklin. "I will bring the food."

"That will be fun!" said Bear.

At suppertime, Franklin told his parents

about the picnic.

"I'm going to bring the food," he said.

"What will you make?" asked his mother.

"I will make fly sandwiches

and fly cookies," said Franklin.

"Do your friends like flies?"

asked his father.

"Everyone likes flies," said Franklin.

"Hmmm," said his parents.

That night, Franklin made fly cookies.

He got out sugar

and eggs and fly flour.

He stirred in two cups

of chocolate-coated flies.

He rolled and

patted and baked.

"Mmmm-mm!" said Franklin.

"Everyone will love these cookies!"

"Are you sure?" asked his mother.

"Sure I'm sure," said Franklin.

The next day, Franklin made

fly sandwiches.

He got out a fresh loaf

of whole-fly bread.

He opened a new jar

of crunchy fly butter.

He used the last of the

cherry fly jelly.

"Mmmm-mm!" said Franklin.

"Everyone will love these sandwiches!"

"Are you sure?" asked his father.

"Sure I'm sure," said Franklin.

Franklin got out the cooler.

He packed the sandwiches and cookies.

Then he mixed up a jug

of fly syrup and water.

"This will be a wonderful picnic!"

said Franklin.

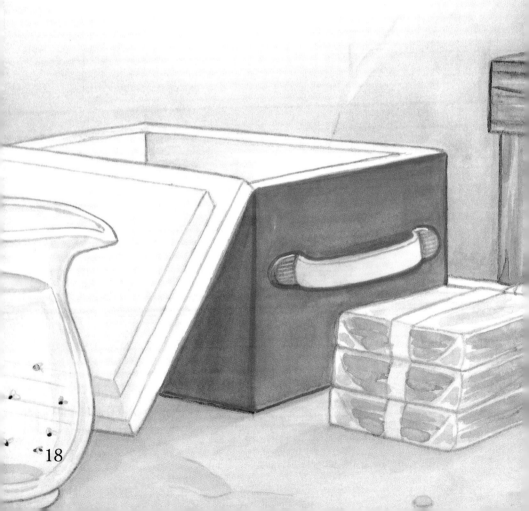

Franklin and his friends

played baseball all morning.

"I'm getting hungry," said Skunk.

"I'm starving!" said Bear.

"So am I," said Beaver.

"Me too," said Rabbit.

"Then let's start
our picnic!"
said Franklin.

Bear spread a blanket

on the ground.

Beaver got out

plates and cups.

Rabbit and Skunk ran for the cooler.

Franklin put out

the food.

Everyone sat down.

"What did you make, Franklin?"
asked Beaver.

"Fly sandwiches and fly cookies
and fly juice," said Franklin.

"Uh-oh," said Skunk.

"I hate flies," said Rabbit.

"Me too," said everyone else.

"I like ants," said Beaver.

"Me too," said everyone else.

"But flies are good!"
said Franklin.

Franklin helped himself to lots of food.

The others watched.

Franklin took a big bite of his sandwich.

"Mmmm-mm!" he said.

The others frowned.

"Oh, come on,"

said Franklin.

"Just try a little bite."

"Well," said Bear.

"I am hungry."

The others nodded.

Everyone took a sandwich.

Everyone took a little bite.

Everyone chewed and swallowed.

Then everyone said, "YUCK!"

Just then, Franklin's mother came by.

"Is anyone still hungry?" she asked.

"I brought a pizza."

"Pizza!" everyone cried.

"Are there flies on it?" asked Beaver.

"No," said Franklin's mother.

"Just ants."

Everyone had two slices.

Except for Franklin.

"Ants?" he said. "YUCK!"